comix

JOKER

Anthony Masters

Illustrated by Michael Reid

My dad's a magician. Read about what happened the day he vanished.

A & C Black • London

comix

First paperback edition 2001
First published 2000 in hardback by
A & C Black (Publishers) Ltd
35 Bedford Row, London WC1R 4JH

ISBN 0-7136-5326-4

A CIP catalogue for this book is available from the
British Library.

Printed and bound in Spain by G. Z. Printek, Bilbao

CHAPTER ONE

Mel's trick was going wrong.

Abwa, fabwa, Oonda...

Mel had never messed up a trick before. But there was always a first time. And this trick wasn't easy.

Go for it, Mel!

It's magic!

It's rubbish!

The handkerchief in the little box gently stirred and came to ghostly life.

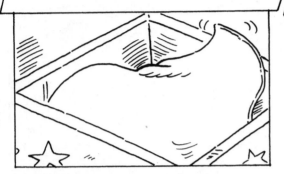

Then it began to stand upright.

Slowly, the handkerchief began to follow Mel around the classroom. Then it leapt into his hand as if it was alive.

The hanky's on a thread! Mel's cheating!

Rather than applauding, Tim Barton was sneering again.

Tim grabbed the thread and pulled the handkerchief along the floor. The scornful laughter went on for a long time. Even Mel's best friend Paul was grinning.

It wasn't magic.

Mel's a cheat!

Mel stood in the bike shed on his own.
He wanted to be alone.
None of his tricks had ever gone
wrong before.
He should have concentrated harder.

In sudden fury, Mel kicked the wooden shed wall.

No one should
ever have seen
that thread! It
was careless!

Mel thought of his dog, Mutt.
Dad had brought him home
after Mum had left.
Mutt was his best friend.
Not Paul. Not anyone.
Just Mutt.

6

CHAPTER TWO

Mrs Jackson screamed and screamed again.

What's up, miss?

There's a spider in my desk.

The class crowded round her. There was a gigantic hairy spider sitting there.

For a moment, Mel seemed rooted to the spot.

Slowly, Mel brought her his bag.

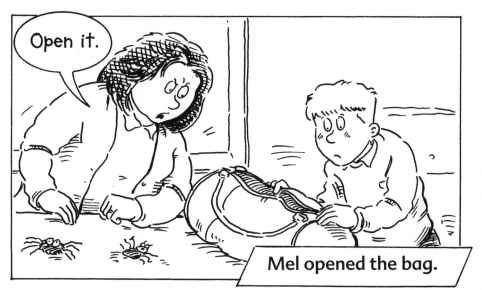

Mel opened the bag.

Mrs Jackson plunged her hand inside and pulled out not only another plastic spider but a couple of stink bombs as well.

Mel stood in the Head Teacher's office, feeling nervous.

I've warned you about showing off before, Mel. I know your mum's not at home any more, but we're all getting fed up with your jokes. They're just stupid. And as for the tricks — forget them. Get down to some work.

Mel was almost in tears.

So what are you going to do, Mel?

Get down to some work, sir.

Mel could see his father talking to a man outside the front gate of their house. Dad looked worried. Or was that just Mel's imagination?

Mel was already lost in the daydream. He was on stage, bowing to a huge audience.

Suddenly Mel saw his dog, and as he knelt down to greet him Mutt licked his face.

Hi Mutt!

The little terrier began to bark excitedly.

Mel gazed at his father suspiciously. He knew he was holding something back.

Later, Mel played with Mutt and then began to rehearse his act. Soon Mutt was walking round the room on his hind legs, barking excitedly.

Mel hugged the little dog. He could rely on Mutt.

CHAPTER THREE

Mutt was on the stage of the village hall, wearing a ruff round his neck and standing up on his hind legs.

The hall was half full. A handwritten placard on an easel read: MAGIC MAX. On the stage stood a large steel trunk.

Mel handcuffed his father and helped him into the trunk.

Mel shut the lid, locked the padlock and tied a rope round the outside of the trunk.

Tim leapt to his feet and raced to the stage.

Tim checked the rope and the padlock.

They're okay.

As Tim ran down the steps of the stage he was still grinning.

Mel felt uneasy as he walked over to his drum kit.

Mel went on drumming for far too long.

Where is Dad?
He should have
sprung out
by now.

Then, from the bottom of the trunk, a Joker playing card was pushed out on to the floor of the stage. Mel froze, gasped in horror, and stopped rolling the drum.

The distress signal!

The Joker card was the distress signal Mel and his father always had in case something went wrong. Mel hurried into the wings and cranked the curtain down.

Once the curtain was lowered, Mel worked at furious speed, untying the rope and unlocking the padlock.

Mel could hear the audience shuffling out. Some of them were booing.

At last Mel managed to open the lid of the steel trunk and saw his father's pale face inside.

The caretaker arrived on stage.

Want a hand?

I think my father's passed out.

At home later that night Mel's father seemed to have recovered, but he was very restless.

He wandered from room to room, starting a job and then going on to another.

Something's wrong. He would never have messed up the escape trick if he'd been concentrating.

After supper, Mel found his dad reading a report in the newspaper. Peering over his shoulder, Mel read the caption under the photo:

CHAPTER FOUR

Next morning...

Cheat! Your dad's a cheat, too.

Mel punched Tim hard and they started to fight.

Finally Paul and some of his mates pulled them apart.

Tim ran off, shouting his familiar chant.

Cheat!
Mel's a cheat!

That evening Mel hurried home after football training. He didn't want to walk back with Paul or anybody else.

He opened the front door with his key and hurried inside.

Mutt was whining miserably and there was no sign of Dad.

Where's Dad? He should have been home half an hour ago.

Where is Dad?

Mutt still whined.

What's the matter?

Woof!

Mutt started barking now and running to the front door.

Mel made supper and waited for his father to return.

As Mel wandered into the sitting room, Mutt followed him, still barking.

Then Mel saw the playing card half shoved under the mat on the table.

The Joker!

The danger signal! Something must have happened to Dad.

Tim began to laugh. Mutt began to growl.

Mel ran on down the road to Paul's house, followed by Mutt, still growling.

Mel banged hard until Paul's mother opened the front door.

Is Paul home?

He's gone to his judo club.

I think my father's been kidnapped. His car's in the garage but he's not at home. And I found the Joker card under a mat. It's our danger signal.

Paul's mother smiled.

There you go again.

What do you mean?

Paul told me you were a joker, but you won't get me to fall for all that nonsense, young man.

She shut the door firmly.

35

But Mutt could only bark miserably.

Mel remembered how his dad had been reading the newspaper the other evening. Mel could see the photo now.

Mel and Mutt ran to a telephone box.

Mel began to dial 999.

CHAPTER FIVE

Mel and Mutt arrived at his father's bank.

It was just after eight and the street was dark and silent.

They waited on the opposite pavement.

Nothing happened.

Then Mutt began to bark as a van drew up.

Mel grabbed Mutt and put his hand over his muzzle as they both drew back into the shadows.

Easy, boy.

The van seemed to wait for a long time, the engine ticking over.

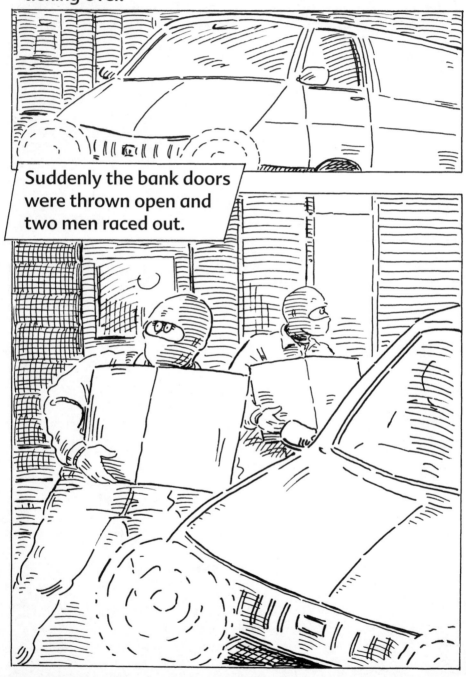

Suddenly the bank doors were thrown open and two men raced out.

It was like a trick. An extraordinary magical trick.
Except it was for real.

The robbers began to scramble for the fluttering
bank notes but Mutt did his best to stop them.

The cabbie got out.

Oy! What's going on here?

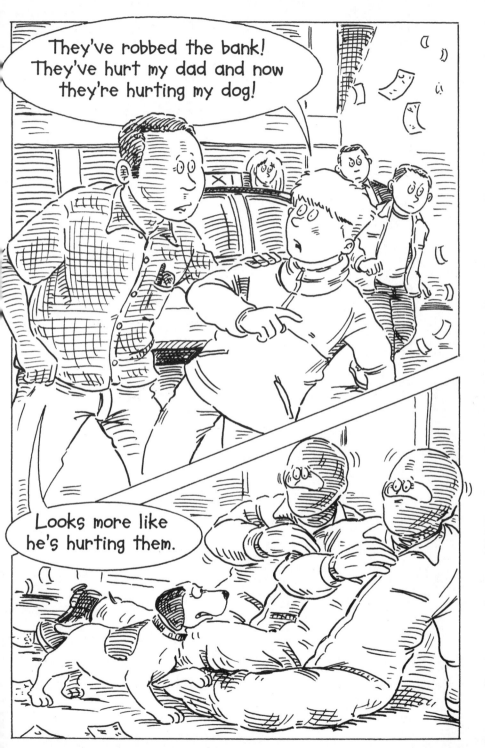

49

The cab driver started to dial 999 on his mobile phone as his three passengers ran at the robbers.

With a squeal of tyres, the getaway van sped off.

Mutt attacked again.

CHAPTER SIX

Mutt held the robbers at bay until the police arrived.

I've never seen so many tenners.

Mutt, thinking it was all a game, kept trapping the notes with his paw.

The other police officer hurried out of the open door of the bank.

It's all right, son. Your dad's fine. The robbers just tied him up, that's all.

How did they get into the bank?

They kidnapped your dad and forced him to unlock the door. Just like you said.

CHAPTER SEVEN

Mel and his dad were sitting safely at home after they had both made their statements to the police.

You were fantastic. You saw the Joker card?

Mel nodded.

I didn't put up a fight.

Dad was still trembling slightly.

I couldn't.

Why not?

CHAPTER EIGHT

The next week, the village hall was packed out.
Mel was on stage and his father was lying in a box
on top of a wooden table.

Mel looked down into the audience and saw Tim Barton walking towards him, grinning.

This isn't going to go wrong.

Who said it was? You're a hero. What was it like, rolling about in ten pound notes?

I was too worried about my dad to think about it.

Magic Max winked up at Tim.

Are you worried about him now?

No way.

Tim checked the box.

He's in there all right.

Tim looked slightly uneasy as he ran back into the audience, who were tense and anxious.

Mutt stood up on his hind legs as Mel began the trick.

Mel's saw made a horrible grinding sound and some of the audience screamed as he cut right through the box.

The audience began to cheer as Max's voice boomed out.

You're no cheat!

The audience clapped in relief as Magic Max clambered out and jumped to the floor.

Slowly Mel opened the box.

But you're still cheating, Mel. I thought you were going to saw your dad in two!

But Tim was only joking this time.

As Mel and his dad stood bowing, Mutt began to bark furiously.